FUMAC THE GOOD

RON SMITH

ILLUSTRATIONS BY HAZEL HADDEN

PROCEEDS GO TO THE KEITH TO DRUMMUIR RAILWAY STATION

www.BrightSparkPublishing.co.uk

Designed, typeset, printed, and bound completely in-house

By BrightSpark Publishing,

Unit 11

The Wards

New Elgin

ELGIN

IV30 6AA

Telephone 01343 544336

Or mobile 07967 178224

Introducing

FUMAC THE GOOD

A VERY LONG TIME AGO A VERY KIND AND GENTLE HERMIT LIVED AT DRUMMUIR, NEAR WHERE THE RAILWAY STATION IS. HE WAS CALLED FUMAC - FUMAC THE GOOD.

HE HAD A CURLY, BLACK BEARD, CHUBBY RED CHEEKS, AND A MOUTH THAT WAS ALWAYS READY TO SMILE OR CHUCKLE, AND LIVED IN A VERY COMFY, COSY CAVE QUITE CLOSE TO A SMALL WELL, WHICH IS STILL THERE TODAY.

AROUND HIS WAIST THERE WAS ALWAYS A STRONG, THICK BROWN BELT. HANGING FROM IT WERE VARIOUS POUCHES. ON ONE SIDE HE HAD A LITTLE BOTTLE OF MAGIC WELL WATER - JUST IN CASE... AND ON THE OTHER SIDE THERE WAS A BOTTLE OF COLD TEA - IN CASE HE WAS EVER THIRSTY - AND A COUPLE OF OTHER POUCHES AS WELL, BOTH OF WHICH CONTAINED ALL SORTS OF WONDERFUL AND MAGICAL THINGS.

FUMAC WAS VERY HAPPY LIVING IN STRATHISLA. HE KNEW NEARLY ALL THE ANIMALS, BIRDS AND

FLOWERS IN THE STRATH, AND THEY ALL LIVED IN PEACE AND HARMONY WITH ONE ANOTHER.

FUMAC WAS ALSO HAPPY WITH HIS CAVE. HE HAD A FIREPLACE, WITH A CHIMNEY MADE FROM AN OLD JUG THAT THE BOTTOM HAD FALLEN OUT OF. HE SLEPT ON A VERY COMFY MATTRESS THAT WAS FILLED WITH DRY LEAVES FROM THE FOREST WITH SOME PINE NEEDLES MIXED IN SO THAT IT SMELT NICE - BUT NOT TOO MANY PINE NEEDLES AS THEY COULD BE QUITE PRICKLY.

YOU WOULD THINK THAT FUMAC USED THE WELL FOR DRINKING WATER, OR WASHING IN, BUT HE DIDN'T. THE WATER TASTED (AND STILL TASTES) HORRIBLE, AND IF YOU DID DRINK EVEN A LITTLE BIT IT WOULD GIVE YOU A BAD TUMMY ACHE. THIS IS BECAUSE IT IS MAGIC WATER. IF YOU KNOW THE MAGIC WORDS, AS FUMAC DID, YOU COULD USE THE WATER TO DO ALL SORTS OF MAGIC THINGS. BUT IT ONLY WORKED IF YOU WERE DOING GOOD THINGS - WHICH FUMAC THE GOOD ALWAYS DID.

FUMAC WAS ALWAYS HAVING INTERESTING LITTLE ADVENTURES. THIS BOOK TELLS YOU OF SOME OF THEM.

CONTENTS

THE FROZEN GOOSE

The winter had arrived early in Drummuir. One day all the beautiful autumn colours could be seen and the gusting wind was blowing curtains of leaves around. The next day there was snow. Today it was very, very cold, and Fumac's breath formed clouds of steam that dropped as frost onto his beard. The cold had even frozen the snow so hard that it had a crisp crust on it crunching noisily with every step that Fumac took.

Fumac loved the cold, clear winter weather. He put on as many clothes as he could find in his cosy, comfy cave until he looked like a big teddy bear. Fumac decided that he would go skating.

Just beyond the end of the railway station platform there used to be a skating pond. This shallow pond

was close to the river Isla. It always froze over quickly as no water flowed through it. Fumac liked to skate, but he wasn't any good at it. His feet often seemed to go faster than the rest of him. His skates would gradually get further and further out in front of him until he fell over backwards onto his bottom. That was another good reason why he put loads of clothes on - to provide some padding!

Fumac's skates were home-made. They were wooden with leather straps. They were big and thick and heavy.

Fumac didn't mind this. He thought that if they could be even bigger and even heavier, they would help to slow his feet down a little.

Fumac closed his cave door tightly to keep the warmth in. He chuckled at the column of smoke rising straight up into the still air from his broken jug chimney. He crunched off across the snow towards the skating pond. The pond was completely frozen, as he had thought. He sat on a tree trunk and lashed his skates on.

Then, with his arms stretched right out for balance, Fumac carefully stepped onto the ice. He took tiny steps. He wobbled around a bit, then gingerly let his feet start to skate.

Fumac was concentrating very much on his feet. He was cautiously sliding along when he suddenly noticed a big goose watching him. The big goose was standing at the far edge of the pond. It was perfectly still. It was just watching. This was such a surprise to Fumac that he forgot to keep watching his feet. His feet decided to curve away to one side without Fumac noticing and he promptly fell over. He crashed onto his side and rolled over a few times. He ended up lying on his side quite close to the big goose. They stared at each other.

Why hadn't the big goose flown away, or at least attacked him? The goose just watched. As Fumac was gathering himself together to get up he noticed that the big goose didn't have any feet. How odd! Then Fumac chuckled to himself.  How silly of him. Of course the big goose had feet - but they were under the ice!

The big goose was not native to Scotland. It had white edges to its brown wings, and odd stripes of white here and there.

Fumac sat on the ice and thought about the big goose. Geese usually passed over Drummuir in squadrons going from one continent to another, to places so far away that Fumac couldn't even imagine them. Sometimes, if the weather wasn't right (and the geese smelled the weather coming), the geese would land for a meeting in a field. Then, suddenly, they would be on their way again.

This big goose was a young bird, probably on its first long flight. It was probably tired. Fumac guessed that the big goose had landed by the water and been asleep when the cold, clear winter weather had frozen the shallow pond and trapped its feet. Fumac tried talking to the big goose, but it didn't seem to understand. It just looked at him.

This wouldn't do!

Fumac took off his big, clumsy skates and went back to his cosy, comfy cave. The peats were burning away fine in his fireplace, and at one side there hung a big kettle. He liked to keep the water boiling ready to make tea to go with his pancakes.

He poured out some hot water into a jug and returned to the pond. Very carefully he melted the ice around the bird's ankles. The big goose looked down and round about. Suddenly it was able to pull its feet up and stamped them on the ice around it. Fumac thought that the big goose must be weak and tired. Without a second thought, he picked it up, tucked it under his arm, and took it off to his cosy, comfy cave.

This was a mistake. Wild geese never go 'inside' anywhere. The poor bird started to struggle and to peck. Fumac understood, and he took it back outside again. He put it down in the space between a pile of firewood and the cave.

The big goose huffed and puffed but settled down for a nap. Fumac wondered what it would eat. He could try giving it a pancake, but it probably wasn't used to such things.

Then Fumac had a bright idea. With all the snow everywhere there was no grass or tasty green weed anywhere - but there was in the river Isla! He went crunching through the crusted snow to the river Isla. Balanced on rocks, he reached down into the freezing water and pulled up a handful of water weed. He took it back to the big goose and put the water weed down in front of it. The big goose was suspicious and waggled its head from side to side. It carefully had a peck at the water weed.

It was good!

The big goose gobbled up all the water weed. It fluffed out its feathers and settled down to go to sleep. It dozily said something to Fumac just as its eyes were closing, but he couldn't understand its language. Fumac was happy to see the bird settled. He went back to his cave to warm his freezing hands to have a hot cup of tea.

Fumac finished his hot cup of tea and a couple of pancakes spread with his home made jam. He decided to go back to the Isla to gather some more water weed for the big goose. He didn't think that the water weed would freeze if he put it next to the firewood.

As he crunched across the snow, with the calm frosty

air catching in his nostrils, Fumac heard a crashing and a shouting noise. It was coming from the dip in the road from Dufftown that passes through Drummuir on the way to Keith. The shouting went on and on and on, so Fumac thought that he would go to see what was happening.

After about ten minutes, he came out through the trees onto the road at the bottom of the dip. He saw a poor farmer and his poor wife struggling with some logs. Their poor old horse was harnessed to a sledge which was hanging over the edge of the road. Logs were sticking up from the ditch. The poor old horse was

hanging its head and holding one of its back legs off the ground.

It was fairly clear what had happened, but Fumac asked all the same. The poor farmer said that he and his poor wife

were collecting firewood
and taking it home to their
croft. As they had slid
down the hill, the sledge
had slipped over to one
side and tipped over. The
poor old horse had tried in vain to hold it back. Now
the old horse had sprained one of its hind legs.

The poor farmer's wife was crying. They would
probably have to have the poor old horse destroyed.
They could not afford another one. They needed the
firewood to keep warm in the winter. What could they
do? They thought that they would try to drag the sledge
home by themselves with half the wood, then return for
the other half.

Fumac felt sorry for them, but he didn't show it.
Instead, he put on a cheerful confident voice. If the

poor farmer and his poor wife would gather up all the wood, he would have a look at the horse. They huffed and puffed, dragged the logs back onto the road, and piled them up onto the sledge.

Fumac stroked and calmed the poor tired old horse. Gently he felt the injured leg. The muscles were all knotted up and the poor old horse was in pain. Fumac didn't want everyone to know about the magical properties of the well water. He couldn't trust people to use it wisely, so he always kept it a secret.

While the poor farmer and his poor wife were busy, Fumac unhooked the bottle of magic well water from his belt. He carefully poured it down the poor old horse's leg, rubbing it in gently while he said the

magic words. The poor old horse looked round, surprised. It did not expect to have its leg wet. The magic well water was cold, too!

Then the poor old horse felt a soothing warm glow in its sore leg! It relaxed and felt just super! It put its leg down on the ground very carefully, but the leg didn't hurt any more. The poor old horse stamped all its feet one after the other and flicked its tail from side to side. It turned its head to look at Fumac and mumbled, "Thank you, thank you, thank you so much." Fumac patted the poor old horse and smiled.

"There," he said to the poor farmer and his poor wife. "All sorted." They stared in amazement at their horse while Fumac finished loading the wood and tying it down.

When the sledge was all ready to go, they set off with all three of them pushing and the horse pulling up the hill and into Drummuir.

When they stopped to draw breath, the farmer and his wife explained that it was all downhill or on the level now to their croft over by Glass.

The cry of a squadron of geese was faintly heard as they flew high overhead in a straggly V formation going towards Aberdeen. That reminded Fumac of what he had been going to do. He shook hands with the poor farmer and his poor wife, stroked the head of the old horse. He whispered "Good luck old pal," into its ears, and set off down the lane towards the River Isla.

As he crossed by the stepping stones Fumac grabbed a handful of water weed from the freezing water and carried it to the cave. When he got there, the big goose had gone! Obviously it had recovered its strength and, when it had heard the other geese passing overhead, it had joined them on the flight to another country.

Fumac was happy - he had done two good deeds in one day.

Fumac was cold and hungry now. He went into his cave and shut the door. The fire was nearly out, so he poked it about a bit and fed some twigs into it. Then he added a few logs and some peats. In no time at all his

kettle was boiling, the fire was bright, and the cave was as cosy and comfy as can be.

THE HOPPING HERON.

Fumac stood outside the doorway of his cosy, comfy cave and stretched and yawned. The morning sun was quite warm. It was a beautiful day, but he didn't feel right. He couldn't work out what was wrong. Everything seemed to be in the right place. All the birds seemed to be chirping away  normally. Then he realised! How silly he was, thinking it was something outside when all the time it was something inside. It was his burpy tummy! He would have to sort it out.

The big walled garden around Drummuir Castle was nearby. Fumac knew that all sorts of good things grew in that garden. The produce was just for the Castle so he couldn't go there. Fumac set off in the other

direction to where he had his own secret garden.
Fumac's garden didn't have a big brick wall round it,
but it had an even better wall - made of stinging nettles!

Just over a hill there was a small Glen sheltered by big
trees. Here was Fumac's garden where he grew lots of
herbs and some vegetables. Carrots were his
favourites. Around the garden was a big thick hedge
of stinging nettles that kept everybody and everything
out of his garden. To get in Fumac used a rope tied to
an overhanging branch of a big, old oak tree. In this big
old tree lived two red squirrels. They had heard Fumac
coming and were already sitting waiting on a top
branch for him. They were giggling.

The squirrels always thought it funny to see Fumac
swinging on the rope. This time they were giggling
before he even arrived. They thought that he was
practising to become a squirrel, but he would never be
able to jump from tree to tree as they could. They

watched as Fumac used his stick to hook the dangling

rope and pull it towards him. Then he stepped back,

took a short run, lifted up his legs and with a big fluttering flurry of cloak and legs he swung over the nettles, let go of the rope and landed in a big spinning tumble.

The squirrels thought this was hilarious. They laughed

and laughed. They darted in quick zigzags down to the

ground and back up to the top branch. Fumac was

laughing too as he straightened himself out. He made

sure that all his pouches and bottles were still attached

to his big brown belt.

Then he went round his garden pulling up a few weeds

and checking everything. In the herb garden, he

selected a few of the best young leaves of a particular plant until he had a handful. He carefully put them in a pouch.

Now it was time to go. Fumac decided to make a better job of the rope this time. He straightened his clothes, tightened his belt, and hooked the rope with his stick into his belt. He could hear the squirrels scuttling and scampering about in the oak tree. He took no notice, as he was concentrating on the jump. He stepped deliberately back... back... and back until the rope was tight. Then he jumped into the air and lifted his legs.

This time Fumac was swinging over the stinging nettles in fine style! He swooped over like an eagle (even though it was a rather round, brown flappy eagle!). He was feeling so proud - until he swung a bit too far and clattered bang into a leafy branch.

Fumac let go of the rope and tumbled to the ground in a stramash of legs, sticks, leaves and twigs. He was annoyed with himself, but he started to laugh as the two red squirrels zigzagged up and down the tree. They were laughing and chattering and bumping into one another.

Fumac waved goodbye to the squirrels, and went back to his cosy, comfy cave. There he put a small saucepan with some water in it onto the fire. When the water was boiling, he chopped up the leaves and put them in and left it to boil for a little while. Then he poured it into a mug and went outside again. He sat on a big rock in the sunshine and waited for the water to cool down.

When the tea was just warm, Fumac drank it. After a

little while his tummy rumbled, rumbled again.
Suddenly, he gave such a big burp that it echoed off
the hill opposite. It startled all the rabbits, who ran into
their burrows for shelter.

Now Fumac felt fine, he decided to go to talk to a
heron. Herons are not like other birds, who tend to be
a bit scatterbrained. Herons stand silent and still and
stare into rivers for hours on end, thinking all the time.
They do not often say anything but, when they do, it is
the result of all their thinking. The result can be quite
serious and important, or quite daft and odd - you can
never be sure which it will be.

The last time that Fumac had spoken to the heron, it
had been staring into the River Isla for about a week.
When Fumac said, "Hello," the heron had slowly turned
and said that the Isla was flowing at such a rate this
week that the water passing them now would flow on
through Keith, down to the Deveron and into the sea a

Banff in 18.36983 hours from now. Fumac had been impressed, but he couldn't make up his mind whether that fact was important or not, so he just nodded wisely.

The heron looked at Fumac, sighed, and carefully unfolded its wings. It had nearly forgotten how to do it as it had been standing there for so long. It gave a tired hop and slowly glided off. Herons even seem to fly in slow motion. They never seem to flap their wings at all. Quite where they will land next, they don't know. They just cruise along until they get fed up with flying, then they drop down next to some water to stare at for a few days.

The heron had once flown slowly all the way to Banff,

following the river. It was curious to see where the
water went. It had not landed at Banff. It had seen the
sea, with more water than it could ever have imagined.
No bird could stand and stare at that much water. The
sea water was all wobbly, with waves everywhere - it
was just too much for one heron. It had flown back
wearily to Drummuir and spent at least a week staring
at a pool by the River Isla.

Fumac walked all the way to
Loch Park to see the heron,
but   couldn't   see   it
anywhere. He decided to
return home and work on
some chess pieces that he
was making. Every March or April the red deer would
lose their antlers so that they can grow bigger ones.
Fumac knew where to go in the forest to find the fallen
antlers and collect them up. Then he would set to work
on them.

First, Fumac would cut out the best bits to make into walking stick handles. From all the bits that were left, he would select the pieces to make into chessmen. Now a chess set has 32 men, including 16 pawns who need to look exactly the same, so it was a lot of work. Fumac made one set a year. Chess sets have two sides, usually black and white. Fumac would boil up some special leaves, a root, and some berries to make a deep dark dye. Half the chess pieces would go in to soak for three days. When they came out, they were a rich, dark maroon colour. When Fumac had selected the bits of horn for the chess pieces, there were usually some antler left over, and from these he made duffel coat toggles, corkscrew handles and loads of buttons.

When the show was on in Dufftown, and especially when the Great Keith Show was on, Fumac would take a big back pack full of his products and set up a stall. He would sell all his beautifully made things easily, and make enough money to last him all year. He didn't need much. Mostly it was for buying flour from the big stone mill at Auchindachy. Fumac kept the flour in a sack wrapped in brown paper inside a stone jar. Then he could make pancakes all the year through.

Fumac sat on his favourite rock outside his cosy, comfy cave. He polished away at the rough bits on some new buttons. He worked away busily until a shadow flitted across him. He looked up and saw the heron gliding past him. It was going towards the River Isla. When herons fly, they tuck their legs up flat under their bodies. This heron had one leg hanging down, and trailing from the leg was a long line of bits of weed and grass. This was most unusual.

Fumac watched as the bird slowly circled, getting lower and lower until it suddenly fluttered and crashed into the tall plants by the river. Fumac instantly put down his things and went over to see what was wrong. When he reached the heron, it was sorting itself out, preening its feathers and fluffing its wings - but it was standing mostly on one leg, and holding the other one up off the ground.

The bird was obviously flustered. It took one look at Fumac and prepared to take off again, but then it recognised him and carried on sorting itself out.

"Someone has tilted the planet," the heron said. Fumac was puzzled until he worked out that the bird was making an excuse for the crash landing.

"What is the matter with your leg?" asked Fumac gently. The heron looked pained and irritated. It stared with all its might at its dangling foot. Fumac looked closer. Some old fishing line was wrapped around the ankle, and one toe was broken clean off. Bits of grass

and weed were tangled in the line, too. This made
Fumac angry. Someone had carelessly left their
broken fishing line beside the river or the Loch. The
poor heron had obviously become entangled in it and
had broken off a toe trying to get free. Very slowly and
gently Fumac untangled the fishing line, trying very
carefully not to hurt the heron. When he had freed the
line, he wrapped it up and put it in one of his pouches
to take back to the cave and burn on his fire. He didn'
know what else to do to help the heron.

Fumac sat down on the bank and thought hard. The heron was uncomfortable, standing on one leg. It kept forgetting that it had a sore leg. It would put the other leg down to balance itself, then sharply pick it up again because of the pain.

Fumac had a bright idea. "Do you like this particular spot on the Isla?" he asked. The heron said that it was its favourite place in all the world. "Right," said Fumac, "Wait here!"

In a little while, Fumac returned with a washing up bowl and a jug full of magic well water. He cleared a space right beside the river where there was a little beach of small stones. He set the washing up bowl in the stones so that it was quite firm. Then he filled the bowl with the magic well water. Meanwhile, the heron just stared and watched and stared and watched and stared.

"Now," said Fumac, "try to get into the bowl." The bird

just stared. This was most odd. The heron stared at the
bowl, then stared at Fumac, then stared at the bowl
again. Fumac said, "If you can stand in that magic
water for three days your toe will grow again and you
will have three toes once again."

The heron hobbled up and very gingerly stepped into
the bowl. It felt quite silly. Suppose some other herons
saw it standing there in a washing up bowl? Suppose
some silly seagulls came past and shouted rude things
at it?

Fumac broke off some big clumps of Rosebay Willow
Herb and covered the edges of the bowl. "There, now,"
he said. "You stay there for three days and your foot
will be all new again. I will come three times a day to
feed you so that you will not have to go anywhere."

With that, Fumac said the magic words and set off back
to the cave to continue polishing the antler buttons. He

topped to look back at the heron. It was obviously not

appy, as it kept fidgeting and ducking its head about

o look at the washing up bowl. Fumac had another

rilliant idea. That made two brilliant ideas in one day!

umac went back to the heron. He asked: "Could you

ielp me with a problem, please? If a baby brown trout

wam from the sea to Loch Park in the spring when the

iver is full of water and flowing twice as fast as it is

iow, how long would it take?"

he heron froze! You could almost hear the brain

jetting going. It pulled itself upright and stared fiercely

it the river. This was a serious calculation that called

or serious cogitation!

Three times a day for the next three days Fumac went to the heron and fed it. It hardly seemed to notice because it was thinking so hard. The new toe was growing all the time. On the evening of the third day, the new third toe was just right. Fumac asked the heron if he could have his washing up bowl back.

The heron stretched and said, "It would take the baby brown trout 2 days 18 hours and 32 minutes." Then, unfolding its wings, which had become stiff, it slowly flapped away up the river.

Fumac chuckled. It was good to have mended the heron so well that it had forgotten all about its injury.

He cleaned out the washing up bowl, and went back to his cosy, comfy cave for a nice cup of tea and some pancakes and jam.

THE DEAR DEER

One morning, Fumac opened the door of his cave. He
could see out but he
could not be seen
because the cave was
hidden behind some
thick bushes. He gently
pushed aside the
branches and walked
out onto the grass. It

was a beautiful morning in late spring. The bright,
bonny flowers were blooming. Chattering up in the big
trees were the birds who were busy building nests.
They were happy because the sun was shining.

Fumac decided to walk up the Strath to Loch Park to
see if there were any herons about. He didn't go in a

straight line, as the ground was very wet where the
river Isla slowly crossed a flat bit of land. Tough clumps
of green grass grew there, as did delicate marsh grass
with its white fluffy tufts. Fumac walked on slightly
higher ground past the walled garden of Drummuir
Castle. The weather was warm, and everything was
peaceful and calm...

Or was it?

Fumac gradually became aware of a noise. It was a
kind of splashing noise. He could also hear high
pitched cries for help! Fumac ran towards the Loch
and, sure enough, down at the far end of the long
narrow Loch, something was feebly splashing about
An animal was drowning!

Fumac had a little rowing boat tied up at his end of the
Loch. He had made it himself so it was not very big or
very posh, but it worked well and he was quite proud of

it. He quickly untied it from the tree stump and pushed off. He knew that he would not be able to row fast enough to save the animal so, after putting the oars in the rowlocks, he opened the little bottle of magical well water.

Carefully, Fumac sprinkled a little water on each oar. He hooked the bottle back onto his belt. Then he held the oars tightly and said the magic words. The oars started rowing by themselves, faster and faster. Fumac held on very tightly as his arms shot forwards and backwards. The boat went shooting down the Loch, leaving a wide deep wake, which splashed with a little burst of spray against the shore on each side.

As he came close he could see that the animal was a young deer. It was kicking all four legs in all directions, but rather feebly as it was tired and sinking. Its eyes were wide with fear and its little head kept going under the water.

Fumac said the magic words again. He shouted, "Stop!" The oars stopped, and Fumac reached out and grabbed the young deer. It was too weak to do much to help. Holding its head up, Fumac pulled it to the side of the boat. With a big quick heave he tumbled the young deer into the boat, which made it rock dangerously for a while.

Fumac took off his warm brown cloak and wrapped the wet fawn in it. It was shivering, and it curled up with its legs tucked under it. Looking round for the nearest

place to land, Fumac noticed a brown head moving towards the Loch through the trees it was the mother deer Fumac rowed over to her and gently lifted out the fawn. The mother deer was nervous of Fumac, of course, and very worried about her baby. Fumac calmly told her not to worry, that her young deer was just cold, tired and wet, and would probably not be feeling very well as it had drunk far too much Loch water - but apart from that it was fine.

The young deer stood up in a wobbly sort of way, tottered over to stand as close to its mother as it could, and leaned against her. Fumac could see that it was getting better all the time, so he asked it how it had come to be in the Loch in the first place. The mummy deer's head was bent right round to look at it to find out the answer. The young deer wobbled about from one foot to another in embarrassment. It said that it had been playing tig with another young deer, and had gone galloping off as fast as it could to hide, when it had suddenly burst through a bush and fallen straight into the Loch.

Having first thanked Fumac most politely for saving her baby, the mother deer started giving it a row. They

turned and went slowly back into the wood, with the young deer so close to its mother's side that it looked like it had been glued there. Fumac watched them disappear, so quickly hidden by the dense trees. He spread his brown cloak out on a rock in the sunshine, and sat down to think while it dried out.

Fumac wondered, and he pondered, and he thought. How could he stop animals from falling into the Loch? It was a difficult problem. He could put a fence all round the Loch. That would work. But then the animals couldn't get to the edge to have a drink. Maybe he could put a gate in the fence? But then he would have to be there all the time to open it.

Fumac scratched his head and tugged his beard. He

unhooked his bottle of cold tea and had a drink. As he was drinking his cold tea, a bright idea suddenly popped into his head. It was a brilliant idea!

Fumac checked his cloak. It was quite dry. He put it on and climbed back into his boat. He rowed straight back down to the end of the loch, tied his boat up to the tree stump, and went home to his cave. At one end of the cave were some shelves full of jars and pots of seeds and nuts and all sorts of things.

Fumac rummaged around, looking for some particular seeds. When he found them he put them carefully into one of his pouches and went out  again. He marched quickly to the edge of Loch Park, and looked around for a suitable place. It had to be where the sun would shine on it and keep it warm. It had to be near the edge of the water and be able to be seen from all round the Loch. When he had found just the right place, he bent down and carefully placed the seeds in little holes that he made with a stick. Then he sprinkled magic well water on them and covered them up.

Every day for a week Fumac went to the Loch and sprinkled magic well water on the seeds. They quickly sprouted and grew into giant Rhododendron bushes. Then with one final sprinkling of magic well water they burst into the most beautiful bright blossom that you can ever imagine. This was just what Fumac wanted. Now, whenever any person or any animal came through the grey green brown forest, they would see the flaming bright colours of the masses of Rhododendron bushes. They would know that they were near the Loch and should go carefully. Fumac was happy and went home to his cosy, comfy cave for tea and pancakes.

From that day to this, no more animals have ever fallen

into the Loch. The Rhododendrons still burst into a glorious pile of flowers at the time of year when young animals might be silly and run about and fall into the Loch.

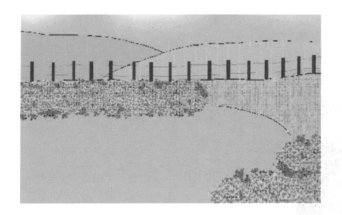

THE FLASHY FLOOD.

It was early summer, the sun was warm and the air was

sparkling, clear and bright. Fumac decided that he would go on holiday. All the year he had lived in the Strath, so he thought he would go to the top of the mountain for a change. He would go to Ben Rinnes.

Fumac packed a comfy quilt and a small tent into a back pack, filled his pouches with snacks and set off. He walked all along Loch Park, through the dense trees in the bottom of the valley. When he came out near Parkmore he caught the first glimpse of the Ben with the other two mountains looming in front of it. From Parkmore they looked as big as the Ben but Fumac knew that Miekle Conval (meaning small Conval) and Muckle Conval (meaning big Conval) would look quite small from the other side.

It was still early in the morning and there was no-one about as he walked steadily up through Dufftown. Onwards and upwards he walked, stopping now and then for a rest and a sip of cold tea from one of the bottles on his belt. He walked round the Convals and finally came to a stop at the foot of Ben Rinnes itself.

Fumac laid down on a bed of heather, rested his head on his backpack and had a little snooze.

During the walk he had hardly seen a thing. The

animals all seemed to be hidden, and there were few birds about. All was still. When he woke up he stretched, put on his backpack and set off to walk up the Ben. The first part is quite steep, then it levels out and the view opens up on all sides.

The really hard bit came next, when Fumac's legs got tired. The last steep climb was hard work. Fumac puffed and panted and gasped but slowly he made it to the top. Up there, the wind had blown away the soil leaving a jumble of huge rocks called a Sgurr. Sheltering from the wind, Fumac spied a gap between two huge rocks. Here he put his comfy quilt and the tent over the top. He made a small fire, brewed a nice cup of tea, and settled down.

Ben Rinnes stands by itself, so from the top a long way can be seen in all directions. Facing into the wind, Fumac could see the snow-capped masses of the Cairngorm mountains. Looking round, he could see, in

the distance, the Black Isle, a
white lighthouse and the sea.
Fumac loved the seaside.
Once, he had walked all the way to
Sandend, his favourite seaside, where there is
a wonderful beach, sand dunes to give shelter
if it's windy, a little harbour, and cliff top walks.

Once, when Fumac was amongst the rocks
by Sandend harbour on a little beach of pebbles, he
had found tiny cowrie shells. These shells are shaped
differently to all other shells. They look like a fist with
the fingers curled into the palm. By looking very
carefully he had collected a handful and taken them

home and put them with his other
treasures on the shelf in his cosy,
comfy cave.

Fumac sat in the warm sunshine,
lost in thought and sheltered by the

big Sgurr rocks from the wind, which invisibly made a

noise as it rushed past. He suddenly became aware of

a crow that had landed nearby.

Fumac sat still and said nothing. He knew that it is very

difficult to talk to birds. They cannot concentrate on

anything for more than a few seconds. Their minds do

not seem to work in a straight line, and they quickly

forget what they are doing. The crow kept hopping from

leg to leg. It was obviously concentrating. Its head was

tipped a bit to one side. Suddenly it croaked, "Tree

fallen down!"

Trying not to look too alarmed, Fumac wondered how

much he could ask without confusing the bird. It might

suddenly fly away if the idea that it should be

somewhere else popped into its head that. Fumac

asked, "Where Tree?"

The crow positively danced from leg to leg and even

shifted sideways a bit before it croaked, "Auchindachy river."

'Auchindachy' - which means 'safe field' in Gaelic - is down

the River Isla from Drummuir. There is a shallow ford there. When the cattle from the far North come down to Keith once a year, they cross the river at Auchindachy, one by one over the narrow ford. The cattle gather together in the field opposite, before carrying on to Keith.

Fumac pondered on this. Obviously the crow had come to tell him about the tree, so it must be something important. But what could be so important? He wished that birds were easier to talk to. Already he could see the crow looking far, far away to some trees near the sea. Soon its brain would be thinking of something else altogether, and it would forget everything.

Fumac asked, "What tree problem?"

The crow froze, rigid with concentration on three words all at once. Then it danced around on both feet at once, bouncing around in a circle with glee at working out the

answer. "Floods! Floods! Floods!" it croaked loudly and triumphantly.

Fumac worked out what had happened. A tree had fallen into the river and was stuck at the ford at Auchindachy. Bits of twigs and grass would get stuck in the tree and cause a blockage. The water would back up and cause a flood at the flat lands there. The poor rabbits: they needed help!

But what could Fumac do? He was at the top of Ben

Rinnes! It would take him more than a day to get to Auchindachy.

Fumac reached into a pouch and took out a pancake. He broke it and tossed a piece to the crow to keep it occupied, otherwise goodness knows what might come into its head and make it fly off. The  crow tilted its head, stared at the bit of pancake, shuffled over sideways, lunged at it and ate it. The crow was so content at having a meal that it forgot to hop from foot to foot... it forgot Fumac... it forgot where it was! So it just stood there like a statue.

This gave Fumac the chance to think of a plan. Carefully, so that he did not alarm the crow, he pulled out the bottle of magic well water. What else did he have that he could he put some in? He looked around, but there was nothing handy on the top of the mountain. He rummaged in his pouches and found an acorn cup. The crow didn't look as if it was reliable enough to carry an acorn cup full of magic well water, but what else could Fumac do?

Fumac gently poured well water into the acorn cup, and then spoke to the crow. The bird started a little as its brain was away in a world of its own. It concentrated on Fumac, who said, "Take water to fallen tree." He repeated it three times. The crow fidgeted. This was difficult.

Fumac repeated it another three times, then he carefully put the acorn cup into the crow's beak. "Go tree," he said loudly. The crow took off with a big flap of its black wings. Fumac watched it glide away, carried by the strong wind towards Auchindachy. There was nothing for Fumac to do but sit and wait.

This event had spoiled the peace and solitude of

Fumac's mountain trip. He was a little disturbed and annoyed - and worried about the flood. If the water rose too high, it would flood the rabbit warren in Auchindachy and drown the young rabbits.

He decided to get up and walk three times round the Sgurr to calm himself down. While he walked and clambered round the bare rocks, he found a beehive, an empty snail's shell and a seagull feather. He wondered it if was time to say the magic words yet. He would shout them into the wind which would carry them to Auchindachy and activate the well water. But had the crow managed to carry out his mission? Suddenly, there was a flapping sound and the crow hopped onto the rock behind him. Fumac hadn't seen the crow at all.

It had used the wind to skirt the Ben and swoop up on the uplift from behind.

Fumac was anxious to know if the crow's mission had been successful, but he waited, knowing the problem of talking to birds. The crow shifted from foot to foot and swung its head from side to side. Fumac couldn't wait any longer and asked, "Well?"

The crow jumped up and down and croaked "Seagulls!" While Fumac was trying to work out what the crow meant, it said, "Attacked me!" It paused for breath. "Food in beak." Then Fumac understood. The poor crow had been spotted with something in its beak and, thinking it was food, the seagulls had attacked it. No doubt the crow had dropped the acorn cup or, at the very least, spilled all the water. Fumac was surprised that the crow had remembered to tell him and gave it a big piece of pancake. It ate the pancake with the usual concentration, and then just stood there contentedly.

Fumac got up slowly, so that he didn't alarm the crow, and went over to where the old snail shell was. He brought the snail shell back, filled it with magic well water, and carefully held it out to the crow.

Fumac ordered, carefully and clearly, "Put in beak." Then, after a pause to let his words sink in, he said, "Take to tree in water." The crow stared at him until the words sank in. It opened its beak very wide. Fumac gently put the snail shell of magic well water in,

and the crow closed its beak and took off, looking very serious about its mission.

Fumac walked three times round the Sgurr again, then sat down. The crow didn't come back. It had probably forgotten what it was doing! Maybe it had swallowed the shell!

With a sigh, Fumac decided that he must take a chance. He shouted the magic words into the wind. The wind took them and rushed them off to Auchindachy.

Fumac's holiday on Ben Rinnes had been spoiled, so he decided to go home to Drummuir. He packed up all his things, taking care not to leave any mess or rubbish, and set off down towards the Convals. He reached the first flat bit, where many grouse were hiding in the heather. Fumac stopped for a rest, and as he was taking a drink from his cold tea bottle he noticed a pair of grouse eyes watching him. Gently, Fumac asked, "Auchindachy flood?" He paused. "All gone?"

The grouse blinked and said, "Tree became twig..

floated away and..." (with an effort of great concentration) "...flood gone!"

Fumac was so happy. He knew that the bush telegraph would have been busy and all birds would know. They chit-chat to one another all over the place, and word spreads quickly. What they say can be wrong, of course, Fumac remembered. Once, when he was at the seaside, the gulls at the little harbour started screaming, "A fishing boat is coming in." They gulls all took up the chorus and shouted it to one another so that everyone they knew would come looking. The seagulls on the beach, however, didn't seem interested. They just moved out to sea a little, to where the waves started to break, and bobbed up and down. By the time the 'there's a fishing boat coming in!' message had reached them it had become 'they're missing a boat at Cuminestown'.

Chuckling to himself at the silly way that birds behave,

Fumac continued on his way home. He wanted to thank the crow that had managed to concentrate long enough to take the snail shell with the magic water to the fallen tree. He decided that each morning he would put a bit of pancake out on the roof of his cosy, comfy cave. Sure enough, the wise crow flapped down croaked a loud "Thank you," and flew away with the piece of pancake.

Reflecting on what sort of holiday he might otherwise have had, Fumac was very happy that the young rabbits had been saved from being flooded. It is very useful to have magic well water!

THE SILLY BILLY

It was a warm, calm, clear morning. This was very odd as the wind had been roaring and howling all night long. The wind had blown so hard across Fumac's chimney, which he had made from an old jug, that it had made a noise like bagpipes just starting up.

Today, Fumac was a man with a purpose. It was late

summer, and he knew that the fierce wind would have blown a lot of ripe apples off the old tree over by the big hill. These apples were an old fashioned variety. They were not perfectly smooth and round, like normal apples. They were almost square with corners on them, and were very hard. Nobody bothered with these

apples because it took too long to eat them, but Fumac knew that they were excellent for making jam. Before the worms, birds and bruises could spoil them, he set off to collect them.

Fumac wrapped his tatty brown cloak around him and took a big sack with him. When he reached the tree he was pleased to see heaps of apples on the ground. He filled his sack and took it back to his cave. Then he returned and filled the sack a second time - though he had to shake the tree a bit to get the last few apples needed to fill it right up.

Fumac's next job was to collect the blackberries. He knew that over beyond the walled garden was a big patch with lots of shiny brambles. He took his big pan and off he went. Picking blackberries is always difficult. His hands and legs were prickled by the fierce thorns, and his cloak was always getting stuck and torn and scratched.

Eventually he had enough blackberries. With one last tug to get the cloak free he went back to his cosy, comfy cave for a cup of tea and a pancake before starting to make the jam.

Fumac's apple and blackberry jam was famous in the area. He would make lots and lots of it. He would put

several jars away to make sure that he had enough to put on his pancakes for a whole year. He would take what was left over into Keith to a grocer's shop in Mid Street. The grocer bought all that Fumac could supply, as his customers loved it. The grocer paid Fumac in sugar and tea, as well as some money.

Fumac rolled up his sleeves and determinedly set about washing the blackberries, and cutting up all the apples. He lit the fire and hung his absolutely enormous jam cauldron over the fire to make jam. Soon, Fumac's cave was full of the sweet smell of jam. The door had to be left wide open to let the steam out.

Just as the jam was ready to be poured into all the many pots that he had lined up, there was an urgent knocking at the door. Fumac thought this was very odd as the door was wide open! So he just shouted, "Come in!"

It was young Iain McNaught from further up the hill. Iain was puffing and panting, and was very agitated. "Please come quickly and help!" he gasped. "Our silly billy goat is caught in a snare, and Dad says you are the only man who can help."

Iain said they must hurry as the silly billy goat was trapped by a back leg and was going totally berserk. The silly billy goat was so upset that it would kill anyone who came near

Fumac didn't know what to do. Of course he wanted to go and help Iain, but the jam would spoil if he left it. Quickly, he organised little Iain to help

him with the jam, and between them they filled the jars in no time at all. Now that the big, huge, enormous jam cauldron was empty, they rushed off together to help rescue the silly billy goat.

Fumac and Iain went up the hill, over the top and down to the McNaughts' croft. Iain was able to run much faster than Fumac. He kept stopping and running back

to Fumac to encourage him to go faster. But Fumac was huffing and puffing and going as fast as he could, with his old tatty cloak flowing out behind him.

As they came closer to the croft, Fumac and Iain could hear the noise. Soon they could see what the problem w[...].in's sister, Myriam, was holding on to her Mother's big skirt. Tears were running down her cheeks as she couldn't bear to see animals in pain. The silly billy goat was trapped by a wire snare, which had become wound round one of its back legs. The thin wire was cutting into him, causing a lot of pain. Blood was running down his leg and he was furious. He couldn't understand why he was unable to get away from the pain.

The silly billy goat attacked the snare, he attacked the bushes round it, and he attacked Donald McNaught. Donald, who had been trying desperately to help, had just been kicked and butted and battered by the crazy goat.

Fumac decided to take off his tatty old cloak and wrap

it over the goat's head. He would hold it still while Donald removed the snare.

Unfortunately it didn't work like that.

True, Fumac managed to swirl the cloak over the goat's head and make a dive for it, but the furious goat kicked and butted and battered so much that Fumac was thrown off. His cloak got a few more tears in it, and there were a few bits missing where the goat had taken big bites out of it.

Fumac and the McNaughts stood back for a moment to get their breath and think about the problem. The silly billy goat also stood still for a moment. It was quite worn out, but still mad. Its eyes shone pink with anger. Then Fumac had a bright idea. He took the bottle of magic well water from his belt. Fortunately it had not been broken in the wrestling match with the goat. Moving slowly so that he would not set the goat off again, Fumac suddenly threw the water over the goat while saying the magic words.

Fumac's plan worked!! The goat became solid and still as if it was made of wood!

Quickly, Fumac dug up the peg of the snare, loosened the thin wire and took it off the goat's back leg. He quickly gave instructions on how to make a poultice from some leaves. Iain and Myriam were sent off to find the special leaves while their Mother boiled some water. Fumac said that they had to hurry as being rigid for too long would not be good for the silly billy goat's heart -

and anyway the magic well water spell would wear off
and the goat might go daft again.

Soon, Iain and Myriam returned with the special
leaves. Donald quickly mashed up the leaves. The
leaves gave off a strange aroma. Fumac explained that
he had asked for those particular leaves as when they
were mashed together they tasted horrible - especially
to a goat. This meant that the mash could be put them
on the goat's leg without him trying to bite it off. The
goat would not like the taste so it would stay on until
the leg healed.

When the poultice was cool enough, Fumac and
Donald quickly wrapped it round the wounded leg and
secured it in place. Already the goat was starting to
come round. Its ears started to twitch and its eyes
began to flicker. Fumac and Donald tied two ropes to
its collar, stood on either side of the goat and waited. It
shook its head, shuddered all over and decided to run

way. Fumac and Donald held on tight. After a

truggle, the silly billy goat was taken back to its pen

nd securely fastened inside. He would stay there for

day or two until he felt better. He gave the planks of

ne pen a few bashes with his horns. Then he tried to

ite off the poultice, but it tasted so bad that he spat it

ut.

This is very odd -
omething that a goat can't
at!' the billy goat thought.
This had never happened
efore.' He sat down, and
hen lay down. 'How odd!

something I can't eat!' This was so puzzling for his silly

illy goat brain that he soon fell fast asleep.

he McNaughts were relieved and happy that their

oat had been saved. With Iain happily pulling one of

is hands and Myriam happily pulling the other, Fumac

was taken into the croft for oatcakes and goats' milk cheese. Fumac liked oatcakes almost as much as he liked pancakes. Mrs McNaught made big square thick oatcakes, so he had a great meal.

Eventually Fumac set off back to his cosy, comfy cave. The McNaughts waved goodbye to him until he had disappeared over the top of the hill. In one of his pouches there was a big packet of oatcakes as a present.

Back in his cosy, comfy cave the absolutely enormous jam cauldron was cold, hard, sticky and horrible. Fumac sighed. It would be a big job to clean it out, but that could wait until tomorrow. He filled it with water and let it soak.

He was very tired after such a busy day. He went to bed on his lovely mattress full of leaves and smelling of pine trees. He wrapped his tatty old cloak around him, chuckling that it was more like a collection of rags than a cloak. Tomorrow he would patch, sew and put it back together again. He was fast asleep in no time.

The next day, Fumac was busy working in his cave. He stashed away the jam, cleaned the absolutely enormous cauldron, and darned his cloak. He was so busy he didn't notice someone leaving a present at his door. It wasn't until he went out for more water that he noticed the bundle lying there. A little note was pinned to it. It read: 'Please accept this with our thanks for saving our silly billy goat.'

Fumac unwrapped the bundle. It was a splendid brown cloak - with a hood! Fumac did not normally accept presents for doing good things with the magic well water. The McNaughts knew that, which is why they had left it there quietly so that he could not give it back to them. Fumac knew that it would be rude to return it, and he very badly needed a new cloak, so he kept it.

He laughed with joy at his swish new cloak.

"But when will I wear it?" Fumac asked himself. "Of course! I'll wear it when I go to Keith with the jam!"

Our Current and Forthcoming Imprints:

BRIGHTSPARK ÉCOSSE

BRIGHTSPARK HORROR

BRIGHTSPARK FANTASY

BRIGHTSPARK CULT TV AND FILM

BRIGHTSPARK BAIRNS

BrightSpark Crim

BRIGHTSPARK Sci-F

BrightSpark Biographies

BrightSpark Noi

BRIGHTSPARK CLASSICS

You can order any of our books from our website - www.brightsparkpublishing.co.uk
or in our shop (where you can also get big name books at 50% of their RRP!), but if
you prefer you can post us this form, together with a cheque for the appropriate amoun
made payable to BrightSpark Publishing, and we'll send them out to you- P+P free.

TITLE	QUANTITY	PRICE	TOTAL
		GRAND TOTAL	

NAME	
ADDRESS	